Pinocchio

Retold from the Carlo Collodi original
by Tania Zamorsky

Illustrated by Lucy Corvino

STERLING

New York / London
www.sterlingpublishing.com/kids

STERLING and the distinctive Sterling logo
are registered trademarks of Sterling Publishing Co., Inc.

Library of Congress Cataloging-in-Publication Data

Zamorsky, Tania.
  Pinocchio / retold from the Carlo Collodi original ; abridged by Tania
Zamorsky ; illustrated by Lucy Corvino ; afterword by Arthur Pober.
    p. cm.—(Classic starts)
  Summary: An abridged retelling of the adventures of the puppet boy whose
nose grows whenever he tells a lie.
  ISBN-13: 978-1-4027-4581-2
  ISBN-10: 1-4027-4581-8
  [1. Fairy tales. 2. Puppets—Fiction.] I. Corvino, Lucy, ill. II. Collodi, Carlo,
1826–1890. Avventure di Pinocchio. English. III. Title.

PZ8.Z2Pi 2008
[Fic]—dc22

2007003945

2 4 6 8 10 9 7 5 3 1

Published by Sterling Publishing Co., Inc.
387 Park Avenue South, New York, NY 10016
Copyright © 2008 by Tania Zamorsky
Illustrations copyright © 2008 by Lucy Corvino
Distributed in Canada by Sterling Publishing
^c/o Canadian Manda Group, 165 Dufferin Street,
Toronto, Ontario, Canada M6K 3H6
Distributed in the United Kingdom by GMC Distribution Services,
Castle Place, 166 High Street, Lewes, East Sussex, England BN7 1XU
Distributed in Australia by Capricorn Link (Australia) Pty. Ltd.
P.O. Box 704, Windsor, NSW 2756, Australia

Classic Starts is a trademark of Sterling Publishing Co., Inc.

Printed in China
All rights reserved

Sterling ISBN-13: 978-1-4027-4581-2
ISBN-10: 1-4027-4581-8

For information about custom editions, special sales, premium and
corporate purchases, please contact Sterling Special Sales
Department at 800-805-5489 or specialsales@sterlingpub.com.

CONTENTS

CHAPTER 1

The Piece of Wood
That Laughed and Cried

∽

This is not a story about a great and brave king, little ones. It is not a tale about a princess.

No, believe it or not, it is a story about a piece of wood—and not even a fancy piece of wood at that. Just a simple, solid little log. The kind that makes cold rooms cozier when placed into roaring fireplaces in the winter.

This particular piece of wood happened to live in a little carpentry shop owned by a Mr. Antonio, whose nose was so round and red and ripe-looking that some people called him Mr. Cherry, after the fruit.

Mr. Antonio had big plans for that little piece of wood. He intended to turn it into a leg for his coffee table.

But just as he raised his ax and was about to chop, he heard a tiny little voice say, "Oh please, not too hard!"

Mr. Antonio spun around, but he couldn't see who had spoken. He looked under his work bench, inside the closet, and even sifted through a pile of sawdust, but he found no one. He opened the door and looked up and down the street— still no one!

Deciding that he had imagined it, Mr. Antonio raised his ax again. This time he struck the wood.

"Owwww!" wailed the same wee voice.

This was too much for Mr. Antonio. He was so scared now that his eyes bulged like balloons, his stuttering mouth fell open, and his tongue hung out over his lower lip.

"Is there someone hiding inside this wood?" he shrieked. "If so, I'll fix you!"

Mr. Antonio threw the wood on the floor, then smashed it against the walls, and even banged it against the ceiling.

"What do you have to say about that?" he asked, feeling slightly silly to be talking to a piece of wood.

There was no reply. Mr. Antonio sat perfectly still and waited for an additional ten minutes — but there was still nothing. "I did imagine it," he concluded with relief.

Taking some sandpaper, Mr. Antonio began to smooth and shape the cut wood. And wouldn't you know it, the little voice came back!

This time it was giggling. "Oh, hee-hee, ha-ha," it said. "Stop it! That sandpaper tickles my sensitive skin!"

This was the last straw. Poor Mr. Antonio was so confused and upset that he fell to the floor, his bright red nose turning blue. At that moment, Mr. Cherry looked more like Mr. Blueberry.

Just then, there was a knock at the door. It was Mr. Antonio's friend, Geppetto.

Geppetto was a jolly old man with a nickname of his own. The boys in the neighborhood teased him and called him *Polendina,* the Italian word for polenta, because his yellow wig looked like a bowl of that cornmeal mush. Geppetto hated this nickname and flew into a rage whenever anyone used it. Of course, this only made people do it more often.

"My friend," Geppetto asked Mr. Antonio as he entered, "what are you doing on the floor?"

"What do you think I am doing? Teaching the ants the alphabet?" Mister Antonio joked. "I fell down. What brings you here?"

"My legs," Geppetto joked back. "I have something very exciting to tell you. I've decided to make a puppet. One that can dance and do flips in the air. Together, we will travel the world and become rich and famous. What do you think?"

"Sounds like a great plan, Polendina!" yelled you know who.

Geppetto's face turned bright red. "What did you call me?" he asked his friend.

"I didn't say a word," Mr. Antonio replied truthfully.

"You called me Polendina," Geppetto growled.

Mr. Antonio said, "No I didn't!"

"Yes you did!" Geppetto yelled.

This happened a few times, the men growing angrier every time. Eventually the words turned to blows and bites, slaps and kicks, shrieks and scratches. When the fight was over, the men realized that each was holding the other's wig.

"Let's give each other back our hair," Mr. Antonio suggested.

"Good idea, my friend," Geppetto replied, and soon each man's hair was his own again.

"Listen," Mr. Antonio said, "I have just the thing for the puppet you are planning to make."

Mr. Antonio went to his bench to get the piece of wood. Just as he was about to hand it over, however, it slipped out of his hands and violently smacked Geppetto in the shins.

"What kind of friend hits another with a piece of wood?" Geppetto asked.

"I didn't do it!" Mr. Antonio said.

"Yes you did!" Geppetto shouted.

"It was the wood's fault, not mine," Mr. Antonio insisted. "And even though I didn't do so before, if you don't believe me, I *will* call you Polendina!"

Geppetto promptly called Mr. Antonio an idiot, a donkey, and an extremely ugly monkey

(Mr. Antonio stuck to "Polendina"), and another fight started. When it was over, both wigs were still on their rightful heads, but the bodies below them had many bruises and the shirts had quite a few missing buttons.

"We're getting too old for this," Geppetto said, dusting himself off.

"Yes, we are."

The two friends were finally in agreement. And with that, Geppetto took his new piece of wood and happily limped home.

CHAPTER 2

The Prankster Puppet Is Born

つの

Geppetto lived in a small, simple house. The only thing rich about him was his imagination. Instead of a real fireplace, he had painted one on the wall. Over the fake fire, instead of a real pot full of real food was a painted pot. It was bubbling over so beautifully that you could almost smell the delicious stew painted inside.

Geppetto couldn't wait to get started carving and painting his puppet. He even had the perfect name picked out: *Pinocchio.*

Upon placing the finishing touches on Pinocchio's eyes, Geppetto was surprised to see the eyes blinking and staring back at him.

"What are you staring at?" Geppetto asked, but there was no response.

Next, Geppetto painted the puppet's perfect little nub of a nose. To his surprise, the still-wet nose immediately began to grow. Geppetto kept trimming it and trimming it, but he couldn't keep up. Soon the little nub looked more like a long narrow needle.

Ducking away from the still-growing nose, Geppetto gave up and started painting the puppet's mouth. As soon as the mouth was finished, however, it began to laugh and make fun of its maker.

"Stop it!" Geppetto said angrily.

And how did the mouth respond? It stuck out one very long tongue.

Geppetto decided he would ignore this bad behavior. After all, he had a great deal more work to do.

As he was finishing the puppet's delicate fingertips, Geppetto felt a cool breeze on his bald head. Why, the puppet had used his brand-new hands to pull off his maker's wig! Pinocchio put the hair on his own head, which was so much smaller than Geppetto's head that half of the puppet was promptly hidden.

Geppetto was getting slightly nervous. He wasn't even done making his wooden doll, and already the creature was misbehaving. Geppetto probably should have considered such risks before he'd started, but it was too late now.

Retrieving his stolen wig and placing it back on his own head, Geppetto bent down to paint and polish Pinocchio's legs and feet. And wouldn't you know it? As soon as those feet were finished, one of them flew up and kicked Geppetto right in the nose.

"I must be patient," Geppetto told himself, "just as one is with a little baby." Taking the puppet under his arm, Geppetto put him on the floor and showed him how to walk. He learned just like a human child—bit by bit, one foot after the other.

Unlike a human child, however, Pinocchio got the hang of that walking business in no time at all and quickly graduated to running around the room. In fact, he ran right out the open door and down the street.

Geppetto tried to catch him, but it was no use. That puppet ran like the wind. Instead of stopping him, as Geppetto begged, the townspeople just stepped aside and stared and laughed.

Pinocchio ran and ran. In fact, he ran right into the legs of a policeman, who did not take too

kindly to runaway puppets. Grabbing Pinocchio
by the nose, which made a perfect handle, he held
him still until Geppetto reached the scene.

Geppetto thanked the officer.

To Pinocchio, he said, "Young man, you and I
are going to settle this when we get home!"

Pinocchio threw himself on the ground and
refused to move. "Help!" he cried. "Don't let this
mean man take me!"

A concerned crowd gathered around. "Shame

on you, Geppetto!" they cried. "Of course he doesn't want to go home, if you are only going to hit him!"

"Who said anything about hitting?" Geppetto asked.

But Pinocchio was quite an actor. "Yes," he cried. "My father beats me terribly!"

The policeman, who took even less kindly to poor parents than to runaway puppets, now came and grabbed Geppetto.

"Ungrateful boy!" Geppetto cried as he was dragged away to jail. "To think that I tried so hard to make the perfect puppet!"

With his father in prison, Pinocchio was free to do as he liked. Running through fields like a wild and happy billy goat, he raced home, locked the door behind him, and threw himself on the couch.

"This is the life!" he sighed.

Just then, he heard someone saying, *"Cri-cri-cri!"* Looking around, he saw a big cricket crawling up the wall.

"Is that you making that sound?" Pinocchio demanded.

"It is," Cricket replied. "And I will have you know that I have been living in this room and making that sound for well over one hundred years."

"Well, it's my room now," Pinocchio said. "So I suggest you stop talking and get out."

"Shame on you," Cricket said. "The way you disobeyed your father and ran away from home!"

"Keep cricking, silly bug!" Pinocchio replied. "Tomorrow I will run away again. Do you really think I'm going to stay here and get sent to school and forced to study? I am going to play and chase butterflies and climb trees all day!"

"*You* are the silly one!" Cricket insisted. "If you

don't go to school, you'll turn into a stupid donkey and everyone will laugh at you! At the very least, you should learn a trade. A skill of some sort, so that you can earn an honest living."

"Good idea," Pinocchio replied, and it seemed as if he was serious. "You know what trade I'll learn?"

"What?" Cricket asked.

"The trade of being a bum!" Pinocchio screamed, laughing. "I will be a professional eater, drinker, and sleeper! So there!"

The smart old cricket sighed. "Oh, Pinocchio," he said sadly, "those trades will only send you to the hospital or to prison."

"You are making me angry," Pinocchio warned him.

But Cricket was getting angry, too. "I feel sorry for you," he continued, "with your wooden head."

In a fit of temper, Pinocchio leaped up,

grabbed Geppetto's hammer, and threw it at Cricket. But, thankfully, Pinocchio's aim was not as fine-tuned as his temper!

"You missed me by a mile," Cricket huffed, unharmed, and promptly left the house.

‿ๆ

As night fell, a queer feeling settled over Pinocchio's stomach.

What is that? Pinocchio wondered. Then he remembered that he hadn't had anything to eat the entire time he had been alive. *I am absolutely starving!* he realized. *Oh, if only my father was here to make me dinner!*

He ran to the fireplace, where the pot was bubbling over. But when he reached out to touch it, he discovered that it was only a delicious-looking painting.

Pinocchio ran all around the house, looking

for even the smallest scrap of bread. But there was nothing. He was positively dizzy with hunger.

Cricket was right, he thought, and he started to cry. *It was wrong of me to disobey my father and run away from home.*

Suddenly, in the corner of the room, Pinocchio saw something round and white. "An egg!" he cried. "I'm saved!

"And now, how should I cook you?" Pinocchio asked the egg. "Should I fry you or boil you or poach you?"

Deciding that poaching would be the fastest method, Pinocchio placed a pan filled with water on the stove, turned on the heat, and cracked the egg on the side of the pan. But instead of the uncooked yolk that Pinocchio expected, out came a fluffy yellow chick, grinning broadly.

"Why, thank you, puppet!" the chick said, stretching and bowing. "I thought I would have to break that shell myself."

Wishing Pinocchio good luck and bidding him good-bye, the little chick spread his wings and flew straight out the window.

Staring after his escaped dinner, Pinocchio began to whine and stomp his wooden feet. But the noise he made was not loud enough to drown out his growling stomach. *Oh,* he thought, *if only Cricket was still here. Maybe he could have made me some dinner.*

Pinocchio decided that he would go for a walk to the village. If he begged, perhaps someone would give him a bit of bread.

It was cold and stormy, not the best of nights to be outside begging for bread. Pinocchio was afraid of the dark and of storms, and it was getting late, but he was so hungry that he set out in search of food anyway.

He ran as fast as his wooden legs would carry him. When he got to the village, the streets were dark and deserted. All the stores were closed.

Desperate, Pinocchio ran up to a door and rang the bell wildly. Someone had to answer!

An old man in his pajamas opened a second-story window and looked out. "Who's there?" he shouted down angrily. "What do you want at this time of night?"

"I know it's late, but could you please give me a bit of bread?" Pinocchio called up. "I am so terribly hungry!"

"Wait right there," the old man said, and Pinocchio thought he was saved. "I'll throw something down."

Pinocchio stood under the window, preparing to catch his delicious dinner. Instead, he felt a shower of ice-cold water pour down on his poor wooden head! Looking up, he saw the old man holding a now empty pot upside-down.

"That will teach you to ring people's doorbells when they are peacefully asleep!" the man yelled.

Upset, the soaking-wet puppet walked back home. Once inside, he sat down on Geppetto's little work stool and put his two feet up on the stove to dry them.

The fire felt so nice and warm on his cold toes. But they were, after all, cold *wooden* toes, and when he fell asleep, a spark from the fire landed on them and they began to burn. While Pinocchio snored happily away, not feeling a thing, his feet blackened and then turned to ash.

At dawn, a loud knocking at the door woke Pinocchio.

"Who is it?" he called, yawning and rubbing his sleepy eyes.

"It is I," a voice replied. It was Geppetto's voice!

Pinocchio was so excited that he jumped up to run to the door. He didn't know yet that his feet were gone. But because they were, he tripped and hit the floor with an enormous bang.

"Open the door for me!" Geppetto shouted.

"Oh, Father, I can't," Pinocchio cried, rolling about, footless, on the floor.

"Why can't you?"

Pinocchio spotted a cat playing in a pile of woodchips in the corner. "The cat has eaten my feet," he replied.

"Open this door," Geppetto warned, "or you will go to bed tonight without supper!"

"Oh, Father, please believe me. I cannot stand up."

Finally Geppetto entered through a window. Seeing that Pinocchio was telling the truth, he felt horrible. Picking up his puppet, Geppetto cried as he rubbed Pinocchio's wooden head.

"How did this happen?" he asked.

Pinocchio wasn't sure. In between sobs, he told his father all about his night.

When he mentioned putting his feet up on the stove to dry them, Geppetto said, "Ah."

"Now my feet are gone, but my hunger still isn't!" Pinocchio finished.

Geppetto pulled three pears out of his pocket. He had been saving them for his own breakfast, but his son was hungry.

Pinocchio instantly perked up. Almost immediately, though, he had a demand. "I do not eat pears that haven't been peeled," he told his father.

Geppetto was surprised. "Are you really such a fusspot?" he asked. "In this world, my boy, we must learn to eat everything, because we never know when we might find ourselves hungry again."

"But I don't like the skins," Pinocchio insisted. "Please won't you peel them for me?"

So Geppetto took out his knife and peeled the pears, leaving the skins on the table.

When he finished with the first pear, Pinocchio started to throw the core away, but Geppetto stopped him. "Don't throw that core away. We may have some use for it."

Pinocchio grew enraged. "First the peels, and now this! Do you really imagine that I, Pinocchio, would ever eat a pear core?" he sniffed.

"Never say never," Geppetto said, and placed the pear cores next to the skins on the table.

Well, wouldn't you know it! A few minutes later, Pinocchio was still hungry.

"Is there anything else to eat?" he whined.

"Only the skins and cores," Geppetto replied calmly.

"Oh, all right!" Pinocchio cried. He picked up a piece of peel, and then a core, and started to nibble them. He complained to himself and made faces with every bite, but before he knew it, he had devoured every last bit of both, and felt undoubtedly better.

"I don't want to say I told you so," Geppetto said, "but after all, I did."

CHAPTER 3

On New Feet, Pinocchio
Sets Off to School

ᥫᩣ

With his belly full, Pinocchio could now concentrate entirely on, and cry about, his poor burned feet.

To punish him for his bad behavior, Geppetto let Pinocchio cry for a while. Finally he said, "I could make you new feet, but why should I? So you can just run away again?"

"I won't run away," Pinocchio said, sniffling. "I'll be good from now on. I'll go to school and do my homework. I will learn a trade and take care of you in your old age. I promise!"

Geppetto tried to look stern, but his eyes filled with tears. He couldn't stand to see Pinocchio suffer. So, taking his tools and two pieces of wood, he got to work.

A few minutes later, two beautiful new wooden feet sat on the table. They were even stronger and faster than the first pair. Taking a bit of glue, Geppetto attached the new feet to Pinocchio's burned stumps. He did this so skillfully, you could barely tell that the legs were not made from two solid pieces of wood.

Whole again, Pinocchio immediately leaped off the table and started to skip and jump around.

"To show you how grateful I am," he cried, "I am going to use my new feet to run straight to school! But first, I need some new clothes."

Poor Geppetto had no money for new clothes, so he made his son a stylish suit out of pretty paper. Taking some tree bark, he made a sharp pair of shoes. Finally, with a bit of bread dough, he made Pinocchio a dashing little cap.

"Why, I look like a proper gentleman!" Pinocchio cried, as he admired himself in the mirror. "But there is one important thing I still need."

"What is it?" Geppetto asked.

"A workbook to learn my ABC's."

Geppetto realized Pinocchio was right. "I have no money," he said sadly. "And a workbook is not as easy to make as a cap."

Pinocchio's face fell. Seeing Pinocchio look so disappointed was very hard for Geppetto. He quickly pulled on his old coat and left the house.

A few minutes later, Geppetto was back. In his hands was a workbook. But he was no longer wearing the old coat. Instead, he stood in his short-sleeved shirt.

"I was hot," Geppetto explained, shivering violently.

"Oh, Father," Pinocchio said, realizing that Geppetto had sold his coat for the book. Running over to his father, Pinocchio kissed him again and again.

The next morning, Pinocchio couldn't wait to go to school. He was so excited about all of the things he was going to learn.

Soon, I will be smart enough to earn a lot of money and buy my father a new coat. And it won't be just any old coat. It will be a gold and silver coat, with diamond buttons!

Even as he thought this, though, he heard the sound of pipes and drums coming from a distance. *Pi-pi-pi,* the pipes and drums called. *Bum, dum, bum.*

Pinocchio hesitated. He had promised to go to school, but the sounds were so tempting. How could he resist finding out where they were coming from?

He decided he couldn't stay away from the music. *I'll go to school tomorrow,* he told himself. *What's one more day?*

On his brand-new feet, Pinocchio ran toward the sounds until he reached a large plaza. There he saw a tiny wooden building painted in brilliant colors.

"What's in there?" Pinocchio asked a little boy standing next to him.

"Can't you read?" the boy asked, pointing to a sign on the door.

Having skipped school, however, Pinocchio couldn't.

"Not today," he replied.

"It says GREAT PUPPET THEATER, dummy," the boy said. "And the show is about to start."

Other puppets, just like him, putting on a show? Pinocchio was crazy with curiosity.

"How much is a ticket?" he asked.

"Four pennies."

But Pinocchio didn't have even one penny. "Will you lend me the money?"

"Not today," the boy replied.

"I'll sell you my coat!"

"And what would I do with your paper coat?" the boy scoffed. "When it rains, it will turn to glue!"

"I'll sell you my shoes," Pinocchio said, trying again.

"For what?" the boy replied. "To light a fire with?"

"What about my hat?" Pinocchio asked.

"That might be all right if my pet mouse needs a snack!"

Pinocchio took a deep breath. There was only one other thing he had to offer. But could he? After his freezing-cold father had made such a warm and loving sacrifice?

Pinocchio decided he could. "I will sell you my brand-new workbook," he said.

The boy refused. But an old man sitting nearby heard the offer and accepted. He knew that he could sell the book to buy a nice new coat for himself.

Pinocchio quickly made the exchange. With the pennies in his hand, and his father's sacrifice already forgotten, he ran toward the theater's entrance to buy a ticket.

❧

When Pinocchio entered the theater, the show had already started. Two puppets named Harlequin and Punchinello were onstage, acting out a fight. They punched each other and called each other names, while the audience pointed and laughed.

Suddenly Harlequin stopped talking and

pointed into the audience. He had spotted Pinocchio. Punchinello saw him as well.

"There's a puppet in the audience," she screamed, "sitting like a proper person!" When the other puppets heard this, they all came streaming onstage to see.

"Come join us!" Harlequin shouted.

With a giant leap and one helpful bounce off the orchestra leader's head, Pinocchio landed on the stage.

Oh, how the puppets embraced their puppet brother. The audience, however, was angry that the play had been interrupted. They began to yell and grumble, demanding their money back.

Hearing the commotion, the theater director came out of his office. He was terribly scary looking, with a long black beard and a pair of mean eyes that glowed like two red coals. In his huge, hairy hands, he held a long whip made of green snakes and black cats' tails twisted together. He swung the whip through the air in a threaten-ing way.

The puppets froze, trembling like leaves in a violent storm.

"The show must go on!" the director yelled, and the puppets immediately went back into character.

Pinocchio started to walk away, too, but the director grabbed him by the collar.

"Not so fast," he said. "You caused me quite a bit of trouble today, and you are going to have to pay for it."

The director hung Pinocchio up on a nail by the back of his coat. The puppet wiggled like a worm.

After the curtain went down, the director walked back into the theater's kitchen, where a leg of lamb — his dinner — was slowly roasting on the spit. Although it was still only morning, the leg was so big that it needed to cook all day. But the fire underneath the lamb was dying. The director needed more wood to finish cooking his food. He liked his lamb well done.

The director told Harlequin and Punchinello to take Pinocchio down off the nail and bring him to the kitchen.

The two theater puppets obeyed.

"Oh, someone help me," Pinocchio cried as they presented him to the director. "I don't want to die! My poor father will be heartbroken."

The director hesitated. Thinking about the fact that the piece of wood intended for the fire had a father, the director found it hard to throw it in the pit. He imagined how sad Geppetto would be, and let Pinocchio go.

All of the puppets breathed a sigh of relief. But there was still the matter of the director's half-cooked lamb.

"You," he cried, pointing to Harlequin instead. "You'll do." The director moved to throw the other puppet on the fire.

"Wait!" Pinocchio cried, surprising everyone, most especially himself. Throwing himself at the director's feet, he begged him to take pity on Harlequin.

"Take me instead!" he cried.

Everyone waited, holding their breath.

"Oh, fine," the director finally said, shrugging. "I suppose tonight I shall have to eat my lamb rare."

What a relief!

CHAPTER 4

Pinocchio Meets Fox and Cat

⌒

The next morning, the director sent Pinocchio off with well wishes and five pieces of gold. He had given Pinocchio the gold after the puppet had described how poor Geppetto had sold his only coat.

"Good-bye, fellow puppets," Pinocchio cried, and set off for home.

A few steps down the road, he met a lame fox and a blind cat walking arm in arm.

"Good morning, Pinocchio," Fox said.

"How do you know my name?" the puppet asked.

"We know your father as well. We saw him just yesterday, shivering in his shirt sleeves."

"Oh, poor Father!" Pinocchio cried. "Well, after today, he will shiver no longer. I have become a rich man."

Thinking Pinocchio a poor, silly puppet, Cat and Fox just laughed.

"Stop laughing at me!" Pinocchio said angrily. "I can prove it!" And with that, he took the gold pieces out of his pocket and revealed them.

At the sight of the gold, two interesting things happened. First, the supposedly lame fox reached out his paw. Then the supposedly blind cat opened his eyes wide with excitement and greed.

The paw and the eyes returned so quickly to their original conditions, however, that Pinocchio did not notice.

"So, what do you plan to do with your money?" Fox asked casually.

"I am going to buy a new coat for my father, and a new workbook for myself," Pinocchio said. "Then I can study!"

"Are you sure you want to do that?" Fox asked grimly. "Studying made me lame."

"Studying made me blind," Cat added.

A blackbird perched on a fence nearby started to say something that sounded like a warning, but in the blink of a not-so-blind eye, the cat leaped up and ate him, feathers and feet and all.

"Why did you do that?" Pinocchio asked, alarmed.

"That bird talked too much," Cat said.

Not unlike a certain cricket, Pinocchio thought. "And *how* did you do that, if you are blind?" Pinocchio asked.

"Oh, just lucky," Cat replied.

"You can be lucky, too," Fox told the puppet.

"You can turn your five gold pieces into two thousand."

"How?" Pinocchio breathed.

"Come with us to the City of Simpletons," Fox replied.

Pinocchio's face fell. "I can't," he said. "Father has been waiting for me. Cricket was right. Children who do not listen cannot be happy in this world."

"Nonsense," Fox said.

Pinocchio hesitated. He had to ask. "How can five gold pieces possibly become two thousand?"

And so Cat and Fox explained that just outside the City of Simpletons, there was a magical field called the Field of Wonders. If you went there at dawn, dug a hole and buried a gold piece, and then watered it well and sprinkled it with a pinch of salt, the gold piece would grow into a beautiful tree whose leaves and flowers were glittering gold pieces.

Pinocchio was filled with hope. Forgetting his father, the new coat, the workbook, and all his good resolutions, he told his new friends, "Let's go!"

Cat and Fox and puppet walked a long time, but the Field of Wonders was far away and night was setting in.

When they came to an inn called the Inn of the Red Shrimp, Fox suggested they stop to eat and rest.

"At midnight we'll start out again, for at dawn tomorrow we must be at the field."

Cat felt very weak and was able to eat only thirty-five sardines with tomato sauce, and four helpings of spaghetti with butter and cheese.

Fox was fat, and his doctor had put him on a diet, so he had to be satisfied with a sweet-and-sour rabbit and a dozen young and tender spring chickens. And a few partridges. And some pheasants. And a dozen frogs and lizards. But that was all.

When supper was over, Fox asked the innkeeper for two rooms so that the group could take a nap.

"And give us a wakeup call at midnight," Fox said.

"Yes, sir!" the innkeeper said.

Once in his room, Pinocchio immediately fell into a deep sleep, full of fantastic dreams of magical, gold-filled fields. Just as Pinocchio was about to reach out to grab the gold in his dream, he was awaked by three loud knocks at the door. It was the innkeeper.

"Cat and Fox left two hours ago," he said, "Cat was called home on an emergency.

"They said you agreed to pay for supper," he added.

"They did?" Pinocchio asked. Perhaps he *had* agreed, although he couldn't remember doing so.

"Where did they say they would meet me?"

"At the Field of Wonders, at sunrise. You had better start walking now."

Pinocchio paid one gold piece for the three suppers and the two rooms and headed out.

It was very hard going. It was dark, and he didn't have any directions. A few bats skimmed his nose now and again and scared him half to death.

Once or twice he shouted, "Who goes there?" and the faraway hills echoed back to him, *Who goes there? Who goes there? Who goes . . . ?*

Suddenly Pinocchio noticed a tiny insect sitting on the trunk of a nearby tree, glowing strangely in the moonlight.

"Who are you?" Pinocchio asked.

Then he realized it was the talking cricket.

Pinocchio shivered. Cricket looked almost ghostly, or at least like a firefly glowing in the dark.

"I want to give you a few words of advice.

41

Return home and give the four gold pieces you have left to your father, who misses you terribly."

"But Cricket," Pinocchio insisted, "tomorrow I will make Father a rich man, for these four remaining pieces will become thousands!"

"There is no such thing as overnight wealth, my boy. Go home."

"But I want to go on!" Pinocchio insisted.

"What did I once tell you about disobedient boys?" Cricket asked.

"The same nonsense you are telling me now," Pinocchio replied. "You still talk too much! Good-bye!"

"Good-bye, Pinocchio," Cricket said. "And good luck escaping the danger that awaits you."

"What danger?" Pinocchio wondered out loud.

But Cricket's light was gone, as if someone had blown out a candle. The road was once again pitch black and lonely.

CHAPTER 5

The Danger

ᥴᡐ

*H*ow *hard it is to be a boy,* Pinocchio thought as he walked. *Everyone scolds us and gives us advice and warns us of danger, as if they were our mother or father or teacher. I think danger is something invented by grown ups, to frighten children who want to have fun.*

Why, even if I encounter some danger, Pinocchio vowed, *I will stare it in the face and say, "What do you want? Hah! I'm not afraid of you!"*

Suddenly, however, Pinocchio was very afraid, for he thought he heard a slight rustle in the leaves behind him. When he turned to look, he saw two dark figures, wrapped from head to foot in black sacks.

Danger! Pinocchio thought. *In the form of muggers or assassins!* Not knowing where to put the gold pieces, he put them under his tongue.

He tried to run, but the masked figures grabbed his arm and yelled, "Your money or your life!"

Pinocchio could not speak with the gold pieces in his mouth, so he tried to indicate with hand gestures that he was only a poor puppet without so much as a penny in his pocket.

"Don't waste our time, puppet," said the taller figure. "Or we'll hurt both you and your father."

"Not Father!" Pinocchio cried. As he screamed, the gold pieces rattled in his mouth.

"Aha!" the muggers cried. "Spit that money out immediately!"

Pinocchio refused, keeping his lips tightly sealed even after the muggers held his nose and shook him from side to side.

When one of the muggers tried to pry Pinocchio's wooden lips open with a knife, the puppet used his sharp splintery teeth to bite the mugger's hand. Imagine his surprise when he felt fur on his tongue and realized that he had bitten into a paw!

Pinocchio broke away and ran. The muggers were close behind. After running about seven miles, Pinocchio was exhausted and climbed up a tree. The muggers tried to climb up after him, but they slipped and fell.

"Ha-ha!" Pinocchio called down.

"Joke's on you," one of the muggers replied, and Pinocchio watched, wide-eyed, as they gathered up some wood, piled it at the base of the tree, and set it on fire.

When the flames rose high enough to tickle

his feet, Pinocchio jumped out of the tree and the chase was on again.

Just when he thought he could run no farther, Pinocchio spotted a little cottage up ahead among the trees.

If I can only make it there, he thought, *I will be safe.*

Reaching the door, he knocked wildly. He could hear the footsteps and breaths of the muggers close behind him.

There was no answer at the cottage.

In despair, Pinocchio began to kick the door. An upstairs window opened, and a pretty but very pale girl looked out. Her hair was blue. In a weak voice she whispered, "No one lives here."

"You live here," Pinocchio cried. "Please, open the door! I am being chased by muggers."

Just then, however, the muggers caught up to him and grabbed him and dragged him away. "We've got you now," they growled.

Pinocchio shook so hard from fear that the coins rattled under his tongue.

"This time you *will* open your mouth," the muggers vowed.

A few minutes later, Pinocchio found himself hanging like a Christmas ornament in an oak tree, with a noose around his neck.

The muggers waited for Pinocchio to give his last gasp, but when he didn't, they got bored and tired.

"Good-bye until tomorrow," they cried. "When we return, we hope you will be polite enough to be dead with your mouth wide open and your gold coins in a pile on the ground."

CHAPTER 6

The Fairy and the All-Knowing Nose

$\backsim$

It was a good thing for a certain dangling puppet that, just at that moment, the pale and kind Fairy happened to look out her window again.

Filled with pity at seeing Pinocchio hanging from a tree, she clapped her hands together sharply three times and summoned her friend, a large falcon.

"Please go and break the rope that binds that poor puppet," she said. "Then lay him gently down on the grass."

Once Pinocchio was safely lying on the

ground, Fairy clapped her hands twice more. A magnificent poodle appeared, walking on his hind legs and draped in silk and velvet.

"Poodle," Fairy said, "please go to that poor puppet lying in the grass. Lift him tenderly and bring him back here to me."

The poodle agreed. But instead of trotting over like a regular dog, he took Fairy's coach. The coach's lining was as soft as whipped cream and chocolate pudding, and it was pulled by one hundred pairs of perfect white mice.

When Pinocchio reached the house, Fairy gently laid him under a soft white sheet.

To make sure he was all right, Fairy called some of the county's most famous doctors, which included the crow, the owl, and the cricket, to come and look at the puppet.

Feeling Pinocchio's pulse, his nose, and his little wooden toe, Dr. Crow concluded that the poor puppet was dead. "Unless, that is, he is not dead, in which case he is almost certainly alive."

"I am sorry to contradict my very famous colleague," said Dr. Owl, "but I would have to say this puppet alive. Unless, that is, he is not alive, in which case he is probably definitely dead."

"And what about you, Dr. Cricket?" Fairy asked.

Cricket replied that the wisest doctors, when they didn't know what they were talking about, knew enough to keep their mouths shut.

"But I do know this puppet," Cricket added. "And dead or alive, in my medical opinion, he is a rascal of the very worst kind!"

"What do you mean?" Fairy asked.

"He is a disobedient son who is always breaking his poor father's heart."

Under the white sheet, Pinocchio heard these words and, very much alive, began to cry.

After the doctors left, Fairy noticed that Pinocchio had a terrible fever. She tried to give him some aspirin.

"Yuck," the puppet said. "That medicine is bitter. I would like some sugar instead!"

"You can have some sugar afterward," Fairy said.

"No, before!"

"Do you promise to take your medicine if I give you the sugar first?" Fairy asked.

Pinocchio promised, but he was lying. Even though Fairy gave him some sugar, he still would not take his medicine.

"You must take your medicine or you could die!" Fairy cried.

"I don't care. I would rather die than taste that awful medicine," Pinocchio said.

At these words, four black rabbits burst into the room carrying a small black coffin on their shoulders.

"We heard you were ready to die," the largest rabbit said. "We have come for you."

"But I'm not dead yet!" Pinocchio cried.

"You will be in just a few minutes, if you don't take your medicine."

Pinocchio swallowed his medicine in one quick gulp. Almost immediately, he felt as good as new. He had to admit, when one is sick, even bitter medicine is a very sweet thing.

Then Fairy asked Pinocchio to tell her how he had gotten got mixed up with the muggers.

"Where are the gold pieces now?" Fairy asked when he had finished his story.

"I lost them," answered Pinocchio, but he was lying again. The pieces were in his pocket.

As he spoke, an interesting thing happened. His nose instantly grew two inches.

"Where did you lose them?" Fairy asked.

"In the woods," Pinocchio said, lying again. And wouldn't you know it? His nose promptly grew two inches longer still. "I mean, I did not lose them," he stuttered. "I, um, swallowed them when I took the medicine."

At this third lie, Pinocchio's nose grew so long that he could not even turn around. If he turned to the right, he banged into the bed or windows. To the left, he hit the walls or the door. If he raised his nose, he would poke Fairy's eyes out. Like most liars, he was stuck.

Watching him struggle, Fairy laughed.

"Why are you laughing?" he asked.

"I am laughing at your lies," she said.

"How do you know I am lying?"

Then Fairy explained that there are two kinds of lies, those with short legs and those with long noses. It was quite clear which kind he had told.

Pinocchio was so ashamed, he wanted to run away. But his nose was so long, he couldn't fit through the door.

CHAPTER 7

Fox and Cat and the Field of Wonders

⌒

Oh, how the vain Pinocchio cried over that endless nose!

But Fairy showed no pity. After all, she thought, he had to learn that lies had consequences.

In the end, however, she felt sorry for him and summoned several thousand woodpeckers. They flew in through the window and pecked all of the extra nose length away.

"Oh, Fairy," Pinocchio said. "I would like to stay here and live with you forever."

"I would like that, too," Fairy said. "We could be brother and sister."

"But what about my father?" Pinocchio asked.

"I already thought of that," Fairy replied. "I sent for your father. He's on his way here now."

Pinocchio was so happy, he couldn't wait. He wanted to meet his father halfway, so he left Fairy's house and set out for the woods.

Under the big oak where he had been hung, he heard a rustle in the bushes and was surprised to see Fox and Cat.

"There you are, dear!" cried Fox, hugging him. "We've missed you!"

"Where have you been and what has happened to you since last we saw you?" asked Cat.

"It's a long story," Pinocchio said, and told them about the muggers.

"Rascals!" exclaimed Fox.

"Of the worst kind!" added Cat.

Pinocchio noticed that Cat's paw was wrapped

in a bandage, but when he asked about it, Cat looked nervously away. Fox jumped in and explained that upon meeting a starving old wolf on the road, generous Cat had nibbled off a piece of his own paw and given it to the hungry beast.

"Kind Cat," Pinocchio said, wiping away a tear.

"So . . . where are your gold pieces," Cat asked casually.

"Oh, I still have them in my pocket, except for the one I spent at the Inn of the Red Shrimp."

"Wonderful," Fox and Cat cried. "Let's go to the Field of Wonders, where you can bury them and turn those four coins into two thousand!"

"It's impossible for me to go today. I am meeting my father. I'll go with you some other time."

"Another day will be too late," said Fox. "The field closes tomorrow."

"Oh," Pinocchio said, frowning. "I really shouldn't." But then, like all little boys with big hearts and small brains, he hesitated and asked, "Well, is it very far?"

And so it was settled. Off the trio went, walking until they came to the City of Simpletons. What a strange place this city was. It was filled with pathetic creatures: hungry and hairless dogs, featherless chickens begging for grains of wheat, and large butterflies and peacocks who were missing their colorful wings and tails because they had sold them.

Every once in a while, an elegant coach passed through the poor and pathetic crowd. In it rode either a fox, a hawk, or a vulture, all of whom looked very healthy and wealthy.

Finally, the trio arrived at the field. Fox instructed Pinocchio to dig a hole, plant the gold pieces, and sprinkle the earth with water and salt. Pinocchio obeyed. "What now?" Pinocchio asked.

"Go for a walk," Fox said. "Come back in

twenty minutes and you will find a beautiful gold tree with two thousand gold pieces as flowers."

"I can't wait!" Pinocchio cried.

⌒

Those twenty minutes were the longest of Pinocchio's life. Finally, they were over and he ran back toward the Field of Wonders.

Greedily, he imagined that he would find even more than the two thousand pieces he had been promised. He would find four, eight, or even sixteen thousand pieces! Oh, the things he could buy, like a palace, and a thousand wooden ponies, and an endless supply of candy and cream puffs!

But when he came to the field, there were no magical golden trees. Finding the place where he had dug the hole and buried the gold pieces, Pinocchio saw only some freshly moved soil.

Reaching up to scratch his head, he heard laughter somewhere behind him. It was a large parrot in a nearby tree, and it was giggling.

"What's so funny?" Pinocchio asked the bird angrily.

"It's funny how easily some silly little simpletons will allow themselves to be fooled," Parrot said. "Did you really think that you could grow gold coins as if they were beans or squash seeds?"

"I did," Pinocchio confessed.

The puppet trembled as the parrot described how Fox and Cat had returned, dug up the buried gold pieces, and run away.

Pinocchio couldn't believe it. He had to see for himself. Reaching down, he began to dig. Surely his gold pieces would still be there!

He dug a hole even bigger than he was—but there was nothing. Parrot was telling the truth.

"I fell for that lie once, too," Parrot confessed, "and I am very sorry for it. I realized too late that the only way to get rich is to work hard for it, honestly, with your hands or your brain."

Desperate, Pinocchio ran to the courthouse in town to report the robbery. The judge was a wise old monkey, who wore gold-rimmed spectacles.

He listened to Pinocchio's story very carefully. When the puppet was done, he reached out and rang a bell.

Pinocchio was pleased, thinking he was about to receive justice. Perhaps those two rascals had already been caught!

Instead, however, two large uniformed dogs appeared. At the judge's orders, they dragged Pinocchio off to jail for the crime of being a simpleton!

For four long months he sat in jail. Then one day, the town had a celebration. The mayor ordered fireworks, circus acts, and, best of all, the opening of the prison doors. Pinocchio's luck seemed about to change.

"Open this door!" he cried.

The jailer explained that only the prison doors of thieves and rascals were to be opened, and not those of simpletons.

"But I am a thief and a rascal, not a simpleton," Pinocchio cried.

"Oh!" the jailer replied, "well in that case, you are also free. Good day and good luck to you, sir!"

He opened the door, and Pinocchio ran out and away.

Oh, how happy the newly freed puppet was! As quickly as he could, he ran from the prison back toward Fairy's house. He hoped Fairy and Father would forgive him!

He wanted to reach Fairy's house before dark, but he was so terribly hungry that he stopped, just for a second, to pick some grapes in a nearby field.

That was a big mistake. As soon as he reached out for a piece of fruit, something snapped on his legs. It was a trap, set by a farmer to catch the weasels who came every so often to steal his chickens.

CHAPTER 8

Adventures of a Watch-Puppet

⌒

For hours, Pinocchio lay stuck in the trap. He screamed for help, but nobody heard him.

Just as he was about to faint, he saw a tiny firefly flickering by. "Dear little fly," he cried, "will you set me free?"

The firefly asked how he happened to get caught in the trap, and Pinocchio told her.

"Were the grapes yours?" she asked.

"No."

"So what made you think you could take them?"

"I was hungry," Pinocchio replied.

"Hunger, my boy, is no reason for taking something that doesn't belong to you."

"I'll never do it again!"

Just then, the farmer approached to check on his trap. Imagine his surprise when, instead of a weasel, he found he had caught a puppet!

"So you are the one who has been stealing my chickens!" he accused.

"No! I only wanted one or two grapes."

"He who steals grapes may very easily also steal chickens," the farmer reasoned. "I'm going to teach you a lesson!"

Taking Pinocchio out of the trap, he carried him up to the farm as though he were a puppy. And in a way, he was. For his new job, the farmer explained, was to be the farm's watchdog and guard the henhouse. The farmer's old watchdog, Melampo, had recently died, so this plan worked out perfectly.

"I am sorry about Melampo," Pinocchio protested, "but I am a puppet, not a puppy!"

It was official, though. The farmer slipped a dog collar around Pinocchio's neck and attached a long iron chain to it. If it rained, the farmer explained, Pinocchio could take shelter in the nearby doghouse. There was plenty of straw in there to make a soft bed.

"And if the thieves come by," he added, "be sure to bark! This is your life now. You must accept it." With that, the farmer went back into the house and to bed.

The puppet-turned-puppy lay near the doghouse feeling very sorry for himself. At the same time, however, he felt he probably deserved his fate.

Oh, if only I could start my life all over again, he thought. *But what is done can't be undone.* And so, slipping into the doghouse and curling up on a pile of soft straw, Pinocchio fell asleep.

Even very worried little puppets who are
being held prisoner and forced to do the job of
puppies can sleep soundly if they are tired, and
Pinocchio was no exception.

At midnight, however, strange sounds stirred
him. Peeking out of the doghouse, he saw four
sleek and hairy weasels.

"Good evening, Melampo," one of them said
sweetly.

"I am not Melampo,"
Pinocchio replied. "He died."

"Oh, no," said the same
weasel. "He was such a nice
watchdog. But you seem
like a nice one, too."

"I am not a dog," Pinocchio said, insulted.

"I'm sorry," the weasel replied. "Of course, I meant nice watch puppet. Now let me tell you how this is going to work. It will be just like it always was with Melampo. We'll come every once in a while and take a few chickens. Of course, one of them will be for you, so long as you pretend you are sleeping and do not bark."

"A nice fat chicken for your breakfast," said another weasel.

"Understand?" asked the first weasel.

"Oh, I understand," Pinocchio said in a strange tone. What did these silly weasels think he would want with a live chicken?

Thinking themselves safe, the weasels went to the chicken coop and easily broke in. As soon as they were in, however, they heard the door close behind them with a sharp bang.

"Watch puppet," one of the weasels cried from within, "what are you doing?"

"I am locking you in the chicken coop," Pinocchio said. "And in a minute I will start to bark."

And that is just what he did, just as if he were a proper watchdog and not a puppet after all.

Hearing the barks, the farmer jumped out of bed and ran downstairs to confront the thieves.

"To think," the farmer said later, after things had quieted down, "my faithful Melampo never saw those weasels in all these years."

Pinocchio decided to keep quiet and preserve Melampo's reputation. After all, what good would it do to tell the farmer that his beloved Melampo had been a bit of a weasel, too?

He did, however, tell the farmer that the weasels had attempted to buy his silence with a bribe.

"As full of faults as I am," he added, "I refused."

"You've done well and earned your freedom," the farmer cried, and removed the heavy dog collar.

CHAPTER 9

Pinocchio Mourns the Fairy

ᘓ

With the weight of the dog collar off his neck, Pinocchio felt so light he practically flew. Across fields and meadows, beyond the tree where he had been hung, he ran until he got to the road that would take him to Fairy's house.

When he reached the spot where the house used to be, however, there was nothing there. In fact, there was only a marble slab on which was carved: HERE LIES THE LOVELY FAIRY WHO DIED OF GRIEF WHEN ABANDONED BY PINOCCHIO.

Pinocchio gasped and burst into tears. He could not believe that his beloved Fairy was dead.

"Oh, Fairy," he said to the air, because there was no one there to hear him, "you are not really dead, are you? Please come back. I am so lonely. Don't you feel sorry for me? You are dead and my father is lost. Who will take care of me?"

Pinocchio was so upset that he tried to tear his hair off, but it was painted on his wooden head, so he couldn't even grab it.

He was attempting to flake off some of the paint instead, when a large pigeon flew overhead.

"Excuse me," the pigeon said. "I do not mean to interrupt you, but do you by any chance know where I can find a boy named Pinocchio?"

Pinocchio leaped up. "Why, *I* am Pinocchio," he cried.

"So you know Geppetto?"

"Do I know him? He's my father! Is he still alive? Will you take me to him?"

"He is on the beach," the pigeon replied. "He thinks you are across the sea. He's building a boat to cross the ocean and find you."

"Oh!" Pinocchio cried. "I must get to him at once! But how shall I get there? If only I had your wings."

"Are you heavy?" the pigeon asked.

"Why, I'm light as a feather," Pinocchio replied.

"What's one more of those?" the pigeon said. "Climb aboard. I will take you."

Within a few seconds, the pigeon and his passenger were in the cool and misty clouds.

They flew and flew, and by the next day they had reached the shore.

"Thank you!" Pinocchio exclaimed.

"Good luck!" the pigeon replied, and flew away.

Turning toward the ocean, Pinocchio quickly realized that something was wrong. Crowds of people stood at the edge of the shore, wailing as they looked out over the water.

Running over to join them, Pinocchio asked an old woman what was happening.

"A poor old father lost his only son some time ago, and just today he finished the tiny boat he was building to go find him. We were all very excited for him when he set out to sea a few minutes ago, but the water is very rough and we are now afraid he will drown."

Pinocchio squinted and looked out at the sea. Finally he spotted the tiny boat, which was by then so far out on the horizon that it was only a speck.

"Father!" he cried, waving energetically, but of course Geppetto was too far away to hear or see him.

Rushing onto a high rock, Pinocchio even tried to wave his nose, like a long, skinny flag, to signal and guide Geppetto to shore.

Suddenly, however, Geppetto did seem to see Pinocchio! The old man stood up and waved.

I am coming back in, he seemed to be saying with his hand gestures.

And he might have done just that, had not a huge wave suddenly come and overtaken the boat. The sea seemed to swallow Geppetto in one gulp!

"Poor man," the crowd sighed. A few people muttered prayers. Then, thinking the excitement over, most of them turned to go home.

But just then, a desperate cry was heard. The people turned around and watched as that little puppet Pinocchio dove bravely into the ocean.

"I'll save you, Father," he uttered the first time he came up for air.

"Poor puppet!" the crowd sighed again. A few people muttered some more prayers. Then, thinking the excitement *really* over this time, most of them once again turned to go home.

CHAPTER 10

The Island of the Busy Bees

༄

The crowd needn't have worried. Made of wood as he was, Pinocchio floated along quite nicely. He could not, however, find his quite un-wooden father.

Pinocchio searched the waves all night long. And what a horrible night it was! It was raining so hard he could barely see, and thunder and lightning filled the frightening sky. Finally, at dawn, Pinocchio spotted something on the horizon: a long stretch of sand in the middle of the sea. It was an island! He was saved!

He was getting too tired to swim or even float much farther, but, thankfully, a big wave picked him up and dumped him roughly onto the shore.

For a while, the stunned puppet sat on the sand and looked out over the waters to see if he could catch sight of Geppetto or any other boat. But there was nothing.

Looking around, Pinocchio was brimming with questions. What was the name of this island? What kind of people lived here? Were they friendly? But there was no one to ask.

Just then, a big fish swam by.

"Hey there, Mr. Fish," Pinocchio cried, "may I ask you something?"

"Even two things, if you like," answered the fish, who was actually a dolphin.

"In your travels around the sea, did you by any chance happen to meet a little boat with the best father in the world in it?"

The dolphin told Pinocchio that any little boat surely would have been swamped during last night's storm. What's more, any fantastic father within such a boat surely would have been swallowed up by the terrible shark that was known to swim that sea.

"The terrible shark?" Pinocchio gasped.

The dolphin nodded.

This shark, the dolphin explained, was bigger than a five-story building and had a mouth and stomach so big he could swallow an entire train. Then, wishing Pinocchio luck, the dolphin turned and swam away.

Before Pinocchio could do anything else, he had to find some food. He walked inland and finally arrived at a small town called the Land of the Busy Bees.

Unlike the City of Simpletons, the streets of this town were positively filled with people working. Pinocchio could not see one lazy bum among them. He felt a little out of place.

But he also felt incredibly hungry. The way he saw it, he could either work or beg for some food.

He was ashamed to beg, because Geppetto had told him that only the sick or old should beg. Geppetto said that all others should earn their keep.

When an old man passed by, however, pushing two heavy carts with obvious difficulty, Pinocchio asked the man if he could have a penny for some food.

"I will give you two pennies," the man replied, "if you help me pull these heavy carts."

Pinocchio was deeply offended. "Do you think me a donkey?" he asked.

"I think you a proud, silly boy," the old man replied. "Perhaps you can eat two slices of that pride for breakfast." And with that he was gone.

A few minutes later, a bricklayer passed by carrying a heavy pail of plaster on his shoulder. Again, Pinocchio begged for a penny.

"Gladly," the man replied. "Just help me to carry this heavy plaster and, instead of one penny, I'll give you five."

"I don't think so," Pinocchio answered. "That plaster seems kind of heavy."

This happened at least twenty more times, with at least twenty more busy bees. Every person offered Pinocchio a job for some pay, and every time he refused.

Finally a little woman walked by carrying two water jugs. Pinocchio begged her for a drink. Surprisingly, this time he was not refused.

The woman set her jugs on the ground and offered one to him. Pinocchio drank and drank until his thirst was completely gone.

"Now if only I could get rid of my hunger," he said.

"If you help me carry these jugs home," the woman replied, "I will give you a delicious hot meal, and some nice cake and jam for dessert."

Not this work stuff again, Pinocchio thought. But by now he was so hungry that he could no longer resist. He agreed to take the job, and helped the woman carry her water jugs home. Before he knew it, he had a full and happy stomach.

As he sat in the woman's house, digesting, Pinocchio looked up to thank her and gave a sudden cry of surprise.

It was as if, with his stomach finally full, his eyes were finally working properly. Although she looked much older, she had the same voice, the same eyes, the same blue hair. Could it be?

"Fairy?" he asked uncertainly.

As Pinocchio started to cry with joy and relief, the woman, who was indeed Fairy, started to laugh gently. "It certainly took you long enough to recognize me," she said.

CHAPTER 11

Pinocchio Promises to Be Good

ᘓ

Because he was only a puppet, Pinocchio never aged.

But oh, how Fairy had grown up. Before, she had been only a little girl, something like a sister. Now, through some sort of magic, she was a beautiful woman.

"I want to grow," Pinocchio cried. "I want to be a real little boy, who turns into a young man, and then, someday, an old man. I am tired of being a solid piece of wood."

"There may be a way," Fairy suggested mysteriously. "For all of your bad behavior, I can see that you have a good heart. If you try to be a well-behaved child, and study and work and tell the truth, you may just get what you wish for."

"From now on, I'll be different," Pinocchio vowed. He held his breath, looking down at his wooden limbs, hoping he would instantly turn into a real boy.

Apparently it would not be that easy.

Pinocchio sighed. "Will you tell me, dear Fairy, where my father is?"

Fairy didn't know, but she was sure that Pinocchio would see him again.

"For now, however, since I have grown into a woman, I will be your mother instead of your sister," Fairy said.

"Lovely!" Pinocchio cried.

But Fairy had some conditions.

"You will listen to me and go to school."

Pinocchio frowned.

"Eventually, you will get a job."

Pinocchio groaned.

"What's wrong?" Fairy asked.

"I don't know," Pinocchio said. "I tried to get excited about those things before, but I am afraid that I am back to feeling that school and work aren't very much fun."

"My dear boy," said Fairy. "People who say such things usually end up in prison or the hospital. Every person must do something in this world to try to make something of himself. You have to fight your laziness! Didn't you say just one minute ago that you wanted to become a real boy?"

Pinocchio nodded, remembering. He did want that desperately! He would try to be good! And he would get things started by going to school the very next day.

But things at school did not go smoothly. Everyone laughed at him when he, a puppet, walked into the room. They played mean tricks on him, stole his hat and coat, and tried to paint a mustache under his nose. One kid even tried to tie strings to Pinocchio's hands and feet to make him dance.

Pinocchio tried to reason with them. "I will treat you with respect," he said, "and I expect the same."

But this simply made the kids laugh harder. One boy reached out and pulled Pinocchio's nose. Pinocchio kicked the boy in the shin.

"Ouch!" the boy cried, surprised. Wooden feet were hard!

Another boy got an elbow in the stomach. Wooden elbows were even harder.

Well, as you might imagine, that was the end of the teasing. The first day of school was followed by a second day, and a third, and so on, and Pinocchio did surprisingly well. He showed up on time and didn't fall asleep in class and even did his homework. That puppet was well on his way to being the teacher's pet!

If he had one fault, it lay not in himself but in his friends, some of whom were well-known troublemakers.

The teacher and Fairy both warned him. "You are doing well and are finally on the right path," they said. "But if you are not careful, your friends will lead you astray."

Pinocchio dismissed the warnings. "I'm too smart for that," he said.

One day as he was walking to school, some of his friends ran up to him with exciting news.

"A shark as big as a mountain has been spotted near the shore!"

Pinocchio stopped short. What if this was the same shark that had swallowed his father?!

The boys announced that they were going to go see the creature, and they invited Pinocchio to come.

"I can't skip school," he replied.

"That's the thing about school," the boys replied. "There's always more of it tomorrow."

"I'll go after school," Pinocchio tried, but the boys pointed out that giant sharks don't just stand around waiting for you to finish your studies.

"Oh all right!" Pinocchio cried. "I'll race you there!"

CHAPTER 12

In Search of the Terrible Shark

༄

Pinocchio reached the shore before any of his friends. When he got there, however, he saw no sign of the shark.

Finally his friends arrived.

"Hey, where's that shark?" Pinocchio asked.

"Maybe he's at breakfast, or taking a nap," one boy said, winking.

Pinocchio realized that the boys had played a trick on him, lying to him to get him to skip school.

"We had to," they exclaimed. "You're a goody-goody. You make us look bad."

"And don't think of kicking us again," one of the boys warned. "You may have dangerous wooden feet, but there are seven of us and only one of you."

"One of me is still better than all of you," Pinocchio replied.

"Oh really?" the boldest boy said, reaching out and hitting Pinocchio in the head.

Pinocchio hit him back, and within a few minutes, a furious battle was raging. Although he was only one against seven, Pinocchio's wooden feet held their own and caused plenty of howls.

Backing off, the boys decided to try another approach. Instead of throwing punches at Pinocchio, they began to throw books.

Pinocchio ducked, first to the left and then to the right. The books flew right over his head and into the sea, where the fish tried to eat them then spat them out.

After a few minutes, only one of Pinocchio's books was left. It was his favorite — a big, heavy math book.

The boys surrounded Pinocchio until they stood in a circle around him. Then the boy holding the math book threw it at Pinocchio with all of his strength. But instead of hitting Pinocchio, the book hit one of the other boys in the head. The injured boy turned pale as a ghost and fainted.

"Uh-oh," all of the boys cried. Thinking they had committed murder, they turned and ran.

Only Pinocchio stayed behind. Running to the sea, he took his handkerchief, soaked it in the cool water, and bathed the injured boy's head.

"Please wake up, Eugene," he cried. "Please don't die. Oh, why did I skip school? What will become of me now?"

Suddenly Pinocchio heard heavy steps approaching. Looking up, he saw two police officers standing near him.

"What's your name?" one of them asked.

"Pinocchio."

"Did you hurt this boy?"

"N-No," stammered the puppet.

"Well then, who did?"

Pinocchio wouldn't say. He was no tattletale.

One of the officers picked up the math book and then looked at Eugene's bruise. "This is the book that injured him," he concluded.

"Whose book is this?" the other officer asked.

"Mine," Pinocchio admitted.

That was all the officers needed to hear. They arranged for some fishermen to take care of Eugene, and then grabbed a hold of Pinocchio and began walking him to jail.

Halfway there, a sudden gust of wind picked up Pinocchio's cap and blew it down the street.

"Please," he begged the officers, "can I go get my hat? If I am to sit in some drafty prison, I am going to need my hat."

"All right," the officers said. "But hurry up and get it, and then come right back."

And hurry Pinocchio did. When he had retrieved his hat, he continued to hurry as fast as he could in the other direction, away from the officers and back to the sea. After all, he had a father to find!

Pinocchio thought he was home free—until, that is, he heard a terrible panting behind him. The police officers had set their police dog after him!

Alidoro (for that was the dog's name) was very fast and fierce. He came so close at times that Pinocchio could feel his hot breath behind him.

Lucky for Pinocchio, he was near the ocean. A few more steps, and Pinocchio leaped up and into the water. Running too fast to stop, Alidoro fell into the water, too. Unfortunately for him, he could not swim.

Alidoro tried and tried to do the doggie paddle, but it was no use. He was sinking like a stone.

"Help," he gurgled.

Pinocchio hesitated. After all, the dog had been trying to hurt him. Seconds later, however, the poor dog's cries broke Pinocchio's heart.

"If I help you," he said, "will you promise to stop chasing me?"

"I promise! Hurry!"

Pinocchio swam out to Alidoro, grabbed a hold of his tail, and pulled him to shore.

"Thank you, puppet," Alidoro cried when he got his breath back. "If I can ever return the favor, I will."

Wishing Alidoro good luck, but still not trusting him completely, Pinocchio swam back out a bit. He swam along the shoreline until he spotted a small cave, out of which rose a spiral of smoke.

Someone's got a fire going in there, he thought. *Wonderful. I can dry my wet clothes and get warm.*

Before he could reach the cave, however, he was caught and lifted up in a giant net, along with a big crowd of fish of all kinds and sizes. They were all fighting and struggling desperately to get free.

Looking up, Pinocchio saw that the net was being held by a fisherman. "Yum," the fisherman cried, looking at his catch. "Fish for dinner!"

I'm glad I'm not a fish, Pinocchio thought to himself.

The fisherman took him, along with all of the other fish, to a dark place in the cave. A giant pan of oil was sizzling over an open fire.

"Let's see," the fisherman mused. "What shall I have for dinner tonight? Shall I have a bass, a flounder, a whitefish, or an anchovy?" As he spoke, he reached into the net and pulled these fish out one by one.

And then he grabbed a hold of Pinocchio.

"What kind of fish is this?" he asked.

"For your information," Pinocchio replied, insulted, "I happen to be a puppet, not a fish."

"Hmm," the fisherman said. "A puppet-fish. I have never tasted one of those."

Pinocchio trembled. "Didn't you hear me say that I am not a fish? Could you be having this conversation with a fish?"

"Well, you are obviously a very smart fish," the fisherman replied. "I will admit that you deserve some respect. So I will let you choose the way in which you are to be cooked. Do you wish to be fried in a pan, or stewed in tomato sauce with garlic and capers?"

Some choice! Pinocchio thought, starting to cry.

"No preference?" the fisherman asked. "Okay, then," he said, and dipped Pinocchio in egg and flour. "Frying it is!"

CHAPTER 13

Fairy Makes Pinocchio a Promise

❧

The flour-covered Pinocchio closed his eyes and prepared to meet his fried fate.

But just as the fisherman was about to drop the puppet into the pan, a large dog who smelled the cooking oil ran into the cave. The fisherman shooed him away, but the dog continued to beg and whine.

"I said, get out!" the fisherman yelled, giving the dog a kick.

The dog growled and showed its fangs in response.

Pinocchio's eyes were too filled with flour to see, but he thought he recognized that growl. In a tiny flour-filled voice he cried, "Alidoro, is that you? Save me, or I am fried!"

Alidoro recognized that voice. It was Pinocchio, the puppet who had saved him from drowning! Surely one great save deserved another. With one leap, he grasped the puppet gently in his teeth and ran out the door.

Some safe distance away, Alidoro lay Pinocchio down on the ground.

"Thank you!" Pinocchio cried.

"You saved my life," Alidoro said. "I simply returned the favor."

The two shook hands, or rather paw and wood, and vowed to be good friends forever. Then they went their separate ways.

Oh, I hope Fairy will forgive me, he thought as he continued on his way. When he arrived at the village, it was so dark he could barely see. Just as he arrived at Fairy's house, it started to rain.

Pinocchio was so nervous, he was afraid to knock. He simply stood there, getting soaked.

Finally he worked up his courage and reached out and banged on the door.

He waited and waited, and after about half an hour, a fourth-floor window opened and a large snail looked out.

"Who knocks at this late hour?" she called.

"Is Fairy home?" asked the puppet.

"Who are you?"

"Pinocchio," the puppet replied.

"Oh," the snail said. "Wait there. I'll come down and open the door."

"Hurry!" Pinocchio cried.

"I am a snail," she said. "Snails are slow."

She wasn't kidding! An hour passed, and then two, and still no Snail. By then, Pinocchio was so cold and wet that he couldn't stop shivering.

Out of desperation, he knocked again and was dismayed to see a window on the third floor open. A second later, the snail looked out.

"I'm coming," she called down cheerfully.

"Dear Snail!" Pinocchio cried. "I have been waiting here for two hours. "Can you really only have made it to the third floor? I am so cold and tired. Please hurry!"

"I am a snail," the snail said. "Haven't you heard? Snails are slow."

Pinocchio couldn't stand it anymore. He had to get inside! He stepped back and kicked the door so hard that his foot went straight through and his body almost followed behind it.

He tried to pull back, but found that his foot was stuck. Poor Pinocchio. Meanwhile, the rain continued to fall. The extremely slow snail probably wasn't even on the second floor yet.

Nine hours later, the door finally opened.

"Whew!" the snail exclaimed, out of breath from her effort. "I am getting too old to rush like that! What are you doing with your foot through the door?"

"It's a long story," Pinocchio said. "Please help me. I'm stuck. Call Fairy!"

"She is sleeping and doesn't want to be disturbed."

"Well, what am I supposed to do?" Pinocchio asked. "Can you at least bring me something to eat?"

"Immediately," the snail replied. The slowest waitress in the world, she returned almost three hours later with some chicken, bread, and four ripe apricots.

"Compliments of Fairy," the snail said cheerfully.

Pinocchio lunged for the food, overjoyed — until, that is, he took a bite, and realized that the food was fake! The bread was made of chalk, the chicken of cardboard, and the fruit of colored clay! Yuck! What cruel joke was this?

He was so disappointed and cold and hungry and tired that he fainted. When he awoke, he found himself on a sofa with Fairy looking down at him.

"Do you forgive me?" he asked quietly.

"This time," Fairy said. "But you must promise never to get into trouble again."

Pinocchio promised, and he kept his word.

After about a year of perfect behavior, Fairy said, "Well, I must say, I'm impressed. You've kept your promise and been a very good boy. As a reward, tomorrow your wish will finally come true. You will stop being a puppet and turn into a real boy."

Pinocchio was overjoyed. "We must have a party to celebrate my becoming a boy!" he cried. He decided that he would invite all of his friends and schoolmates.

Fairy promised to prepare two hundred cups of hot chocolate and four hundred pieces of cake with whipped cream.

Oh, what a party it was going to be!

CHAPTER 14

A "But" Instead of Boy

❧

All seemed to be settled. Pinocchio had finally proven himself and was now ready to become a boy!

However, in a certain puppet's life, there was always a "but," bound to spoil everything.

"Can I go hand out invitations?" Pinocchio asked Fairy.

"Of course," Fairy replied. "But be sure to be home before dark."

"I promise," Pinocchio said.

"It is easy to give a promise," Fairy warned, "but not always so easy to keep it."

"It's a cinch!" Pinocchio declared confidently.

"We'll see," Fairy said.

Pinocchio ran around town and, within an hour, handed out all of his invitations but one: Lamp-Wick's.

Lamp-Wick was Pinocchio's best friend. His real name was Romeo, but everyone called him Lamp-Wick because of his long, thin, stringlike face. He was the laziest boy in school, but Pinocchio still loved him.

It took a very long time, but finally Pinocchio found Lamp-Wick hiding in an alley. Lamp-Wick explained that he was waiting until sunset, at which point he planned to run far, far away.

"How?" Pinocchio asked.

"A wagon is going to come by and I am going to hop on," Lamp-Wick explained.

"But haven't you heard?" Pinocchio asked. "Tomorrow, I am going to become a real boy. I'm having a party and you have to come."

"Terribly sorry," Lamp-Wick said, "but I told you, I leave tonight for Funland. It is a magical land, with no schools, teachers, or books. Every day is Saturday, except Sunday. All you do is play. You should come, too."

Pinocchio had to admit, this magical place called Funland sounded wonderful. But he had made Fairy a promise, and he was about to become a boy!

Just then he also recalled his additional promise to Fairy that he would return home before dark. And the sun was starting to set.

"I've got to go!" he cried. "Fairy will scold me!"

"Let her scold," scoffed Lamp-wick. "After a few minutes, she will get tired and stop."

Pinocchio considered that. Then he asked,

"Are there really no schools in this Funland place? Not even the shadow of a school?"

"Not a one."

Both boys watched as the sun dipped below the horizon.

"It is dark already," Lamp-wick pointed out. "You're already in trouble."

The boys could hear the wheels of an approaching wagon in the distance.

"Well . . ." that rascal Pinocchio said.

When the wagon arrived, twelve pairs of donkeys were pulling it. Each one was a different color, and they were all wearing sneakers!

The driver was a round, shiny little man with a big friendly smile.

"Climb aboard, boys!" he cried.

But the wagon was so packed with other boys that it looked like a can of sardines. There was simply no room.

"I'll sit up front with you," Lamp-Wick said to the driver.

"And what about you?" the driver asked Pinocchio.

"I'll just stay behind," Pinocchio said. "It's for the best. I'll just go home and study."

"No!" cried Lamp-Wick and all of the other bad boys. "Come with us and we'll always be happy! We can play with toys and make lots of noise from morning until night!"

"Well . . ." Pinocchio said, wavering. "Okay, but there's no room for me!"

"You can ride one of the donkeys," the driver said.

And climbing aboard, Pinocchio did just that. But as the donkeys galloped along the bumpy road, Pinocchio imagined he heard a very quiet voice whispering to him: "You are making a mistake."

After about a mile or so, Pinocchio heard the whispering again. "Oh, silly simpleton," it said.

"Boys who run away from home and school can only come to no good. Someday you will realize that, but it will be too late."

Spooked, Pinocchio jumped off of the donkey he had been riding and ran around to look him in the face.

"Did you say something?" he asked.

The donkey just stared at him blankly. But did Pinocchio imagine it, or was the donkey crying?

"Don't you worry about that dumb animal," the driver snapped. "Climb back on and let's get on our way."

Pinocchio obeyed and the wagon resumed its journey. The next morning, they finally reached the magical land of fun.

And what a place it was! It was entirely composed of boys and toys. Everywhere you looked, boys were playing. Some played marbles, others hopscotch or basketball. Some played tag, and others did handstands.

The boys couldn't be happier! The weeks passed by like lightning.

"And to think," Lamp-Wick said to Pinocchio, "you were going to stay home and miss all this."

"And to think, Teacher told me you were a bad influence," Pinocchio added.

The fun times continued, and the months passed. One morning, however, Pinocchio woke up to a surprise. His ears had turned into donkey ears! They were at least ten inches long, and as hairy and gray as shoe brushes!

He started to cry bitterly. Upon hearing the sobs, a fat little squirrel came into the room.

"Oh," she said, nodding. "I see you have the fever."

"What fever?"

The squirrel shook her head sadly. "The Donkey Fever."

"I've never heard of it. Is it serious?"

The squirrel told Pinocchio that in three

hours, he would no longer be a puppet or a boy, but would turn completely into a donkey!

"How did this happen?" Pinocchio asked.

"It is what happens to all boys who hate books and schools and teachers, and who spend their days concerned only with fun," the squirrel explained.

"But it's not my fault!" Pinocchio cried. "Lamp-Wick is the one who suggested I come here. He is a horrible influence!"

Pinocchio was determined to go find Lamp-Wick and give him a piece of his mind. Putting a large cotton bag with eyeholes over his head to hide those horrible donkey ears, Pinocchio got ready to go.

When he reached the door and opened it, however, his friend was standing right there. Lamp-Wick had come to him, and he, too, was wearing a cotton bag over his head. Could it be . . . ?

"Why are you wearing that bag?" Pinocchio demanded.

"You answer first," Lamp-Wick said.

"I, um, bruised my knee," Pinocchio said.

"I stubbed my toe," Lamp-Wick replied.

After a few minutes of not meeting each others' eyes, Pinocchio finally spoke up. "Tell me, Lamp-Wick," he said, "might you be suffering from a sort of, um, earache?"

"I might be," Lamp-Wick replied. "You too?"

The boys agreed that on the count of three, they would pull off their cotton bags and reveal themselves.

On "three," the bags came off, and—wouldn't you know it—both boys stood there with identical donkey ears!

It was so ridiculous that they had to laugh. The laughter soon stopped, however, when other parts of their bodies began to change. As they watched in horror, their arms turned into long hairy legs and their faces lengthened into snouts. Their backs became broader and grew

long bristles. Then, worst of all, both of them grew long donkey tails!

Pinocchio opened his mouth to say something, but all that came out was a donkey bray!

"Haw! Haw!" Lamp-Wick replied.

At that moment, there was a loud knock at the door. Who could it be?

CHAPTER 15

Pinocchio Gets Sold to the Circus

~⌀~

"Who is it?" the boys-turned-donkeys brayed politely.

"It is the driver of the wagon that brought you here. Open this door or I'll kick it in."

He seemed to understand their strange new language. And without even giving them a chance to open the door, kick it in he did.

"Hello, boys," the round man said, still smiling. He didn't seem surprised at all. "Or should I say donkeys?" Putting bridles on them both, he started to pull them out the door.

"Where are we going?" Lamp-Wicked tried to say, or bray.

The driver was taking the boys to market, and not to buy them some lovely snacks, either. No, he told them: He was taking them there to sell them!

It turned out that the driver of the wagon had another profession, that of donkey dealer. He went around the world looking for lazy boys — those who ran away from home and from school and were therefore destined to become donkeys. He made quite a good living doing this. There were, it seemed, many such boys around!

At the market, Lamp-Wick was bought by a farmer, and Pinocchio went to the owner of a circus, known to be a mean and greedy man.

The next morning, Pinocchio's new job began. The circus owner was determined to teach his new donkey how to jump and bow, dance a waltz and a polka, and even stand on his head. Oh, how the crowds would laugh! How rich the circus owner would become!

Pinocchio worked hard and finally mastered all of the tricks. The circus could open at last.

The circus owner went around town and posted signs announcing the FIRST PUBLIC APPEARANCE OF THE FAMOUS DANCING DONKEY CALLED PINOCCHIO.

As you might imagine, that night the stands were filled to overflowing. Everyone wanted to see the dancing donkey.

Standing in the center of the ring, the circus owner cleared his throat and lifted up his microphone.

"Ladies and Gentleman," he said. "Boys and girls. You are in for a wonderful night, for soon you shall meet the world famous Donkey of the Dance!"

The audience clapped politely.

"I found this donkey in the wilds of Africa,"

the circus owner continued. "And what a savage violent beast he was. It took all of my will to tame him! But tame him I did. And I now present to you . . . Pinocchio!"

This was Pinocchio's cue to enter the ring. Upon spotting him, the audience erupted in applause.

Oh, what a dolled up donkey he was. The circus owner had dressed him up with a new bridle of shining leather and polished brass buckles. Pretty flowers and ribbons decorated his braided mane and tail, and a great sash of gold and silver was fastened around his waist.

The circus owner gave Pinocchio the signal, and Pinocchio began to perform. He knew the drills. First he had to walk around the ring. Then, at the sound of the owner's whistle, he was to change to a trot. The trot was to be followed by a gallop, and then, finally, a full-speed run.

All of a sudden, the owner raised his arm and

shot a pistol into the air. The audience gasped—
some people even screamed—especially when
they saw that the famous dancing donkey had
fallen down, as if dead!

They needn't have worried, though. Playing
dead was just another one of the famous donkey's
tricks. At the owner's signal, the donkey leaped
back up to his feet and took a bow.

When he raised his head, Pinocchio saw a
beautiful woman in the stands. Around her neck,
she wore a medallion with a picture of a puppet
painted on it.

The picture was of him, Pinocchio realized!
And the woman was Fairy!

"Fairy!" he tried to cry out, but because he was
a donkey, the word came out as a horrible, honk-
ing bray. The audience laughed, and Pinocchio
looked down in shame. When he lifted his head
again, Fairy was gone.

The circus owner cracked his whip and

Pinocchio knew it was time to jump through some hoops.

Although he had practiced several times, he was so sad about Fairy that he didn't feel like jumping. Instead, each time he came near the hoop, he decided to go under it instead.

The circus owner screamed at him. Pinocchio tried to jump through the next hoop, but he was so distracted that he tripped and fell. He hurt his leg and limped to the side of the ring. The show, it seemed, was over.

The doctor was called to examine Pinocchio, and he declared that the donkey would be lame for the rest of his life.

"What would I want with a lame donkey?" the owner asked angrily.

The next day, the owner came to Pinocchio's stall, put a bridle around his neck, and roughly pulled him out.

"I am taking this useless beast to the market

to sell it," the owner muttered to himself, and pulled the donkey forward.

"Not if I have anything to say about it!" Pinocchio brayed stubbornly. After all, what if his next owner turned out to be even meaner than the circus owner?

Pinocchio quickly pulled away from the circus owner and, even though his leg still hurt, ran like lightning.

CHAPTER 16

Pinocchio Meets the Shark

Pinocchio ran so fast that, upon reaching a cliff next to the sea, he couldn't stop. He plunged right over the edge!

He inhaled a great deal of water and thought he would drown. And perhaps he would have, had a thousand fish not suddenly surrounded him—sent, they said, by Fairy.

The fish began to nibble on his ears, his nose, his neck, and his mane. One fish even did him the great favor of eating his hairy tail.

When the fish were done eating all the meat, they came to the bones—or rather, in Pinocchio's case, to the wood that the puppet was made of. But it was very hard wood—the kind that gave fish indigestion—and so they swam away and the puppet was saved.

Pinocchio was a light and bouncy puppet once more, and he turned and started to swim out to sea.

Soon he spotted a large white rock in the middle of the sea. On the rock stood a little blue goat, bleating and beckoning to the puppet.

Something about the goat seemed familiar. It was her blue hair, Pinocchio realized. It reminded him of Fairy's! Kicking his legs even harder, he speed-swam toward the rock to greet her.

Just then, however, a horrible sea monster with a huge head lunged out of the water in front of him.

Do you know what it was? None other than

the enormous shark that has already been mentioned in this story.

"Look out!" bleated the little blue goat. And Pinocchio tried to look out. He swam and kicked as hard as he could, but it was no use. The monster opened its mouth and Pinocchio disappeared into it.

Pinocchio found himself resting on the shark's tongue, in between three rows of gleaming white teeth.

A second later, however, and without even chewing him first, the shark swallowed the tiny puppet as easily as if he were a pill. He sucked Pinocchio down deep into his stomach with one satisfied gulp.

Pinocchio must have fainted from fear, or hit his hard wooden head during the fall. When he awoke, he could not remember where he was.

It was pitch-black in that shark's stomach. Once in a while, a cold breeze blew. Some time later, Pinocchio remembered what had happened and realized that the breeze was from the shark breathing. (The poor shark was suffering from asthma, so it was some breeze!)

Pinocchio burst into tears. "Help! Help!" he cried. "Oh, poor me! Won't someone come to save me?"

"And who do you think will hear and help you in here?" asked a rough gravelly voice beside Pinocchio.

"Who's there?" Pinocchio whispered.

It turned out that the voice belonged to a poor tunny fish, which had also been swallowed by the shark.

"What kind of fish are you?" the tunny fish asked.

"What are we going to do?" Pinocchio replied, ignoring the question.

"Wait until the shark has digested us both, I suppose," the tunny fish said in a resigned voice.

"But I don't want to be digested," shouted Pinocchio, starting to sob.

"Well neither do I," said the tunny. "But I suppose dying this way is more dignified than being fried up in a pan."

Pinocchio guessed that the tunny was right, and he was certainly grateful that he was no longer covered in flour. But unlike the tunny, he refused to give up so easily.

Just then, about a mile in the distance, Pinocchio thought he saw a faint light.

Thinking that he might find some other poor swallowed soul, possibly a wise old fish who might know how to escape, Pinocchio vowed to reach the light.

"Come with me," Pinocchio suggested.

"No," the tunny sighed. "I'm too scared to try. Good luck and good-bye!"

CHAPTER 17

Pinocchio Finds His Father!

～

Pinocchio walked for what felt like miles to get to the source of the light.

Finally he found it, and can you guess what it was? A candle stuck in a glass bottle, sitting on a table. At the table sat not a fish, but a little old man munching on something.

Pinocchio squinted and looked closer. Wait—could it possibly be? He wanted to laugh, he wanted to cry, he wanted to say a thousand and one things, but all he could do was stand still, stuttering and stammering brokenly.

126

At last, with a great effort, he opened his arms wide and ran, rushing to embrace the little old man.

"Father! I have found you at last!"

The old man rubbed his eyes.

"Could it possibly be?" he stammered and blinked. "Are you really my dear little Pinocchio?"

Pinocchio assured him that indeed, he was. Sitting on his father's lap, he then proceeded to tell him, in an excited rush, everything that had happened to him since they had parted ways.

"I saw you when you swam out to reach me!" Geppetto exclaimed. "But I couldn't get the boat back to shore. The waves were so rough, and then this terrible shark came and swallowed me."

"And you have been here, in the shark's stomach, for these past two years?" Pinocchio asked, amazed. "How have you survived?"

Geppetto explained that the shark had also swallowed a large sunken ship, free of sailors, but loaded with meat, canned goods, crackers, raisins, cheese, coffee, sugar, candles, and matches.

"Unfortunately," Geppetto said, "I am down to my final crumbs and my very last candle."

"And then?"

"And then, my son, we shall find ourselves sitting in darkness."

"Then there is no time to lose!" Pinocchio cried. "We must try to escape!

Pinocchio suggested that they run out of the shark's mouth and dive into the sea, but Geppetto, like the tunny, was scared and unsure.

"I can't swim," he added.

"Well I can," Pinocchio replied. "I will carry you on my shoulders! Don't be afraid. Come on!"

Father and son walked a long while through the stomach and the whole body of the shark. When they reached the throat, they stopped and hid behind a tonsil, waiting for just the right moment to make their move.

That poor old asthmatic shark slept with its mouth open in order to breathe. Pinocchio could look out and see the starry sky.

Grabbing Geppetto's hand, Pinocchio whispered, "Now!"

The two climbed up the throat, walking carefully on their tiptoes across the shark's thick spongy tongue, trying not to tickle him.

But tickle him they must have for, at that moment, the shark gave a terrible wheeze, violently sucking them back down into his stomach.

To make matters worse, the candle had now gone out and the two were left in darkness.

"Oh well," Geppetto said. "We tried."

"And we will try again!" Pinocchio vowed. "Give me your hand, dear Father, and don't be scared."

With these words, Pinocchio led his father back up the throat, across the tongue, and carefully over three rows of teeth.

At the edge of the shark's mouth, Pinocchio told his father to climb aboard. With Geppetto seated comfortably on his shoulders, Pinocchio did a swan dive into the ocean and began to swim.

The sea was smooth, and the moon lit their way. Finally they were free, reunited and headed home.

Everything seemed fine, until Pinocchio noticed that his father was shivering violently in the cold water.

"Hang in there," Pinocchio said. "We're almost at the shore."

Geppetto weakly lifted up his head. "I see nothing but sea and sky."

Pinocchio had to admit that his father was right. And he, himself, was getting weak and starting to shiver from the cold of the water. Still, he tried to comfort the old man.

"I see it," he lied. And this time, perhaps

because his lie was for a very good cause, his nose stayed put.

Pinocchio continued to try his best. Soon, however, he could not fake it any longer. He was exhausted, too. It was over.

"I'm so sorry, Father," he whispered, his head just barely above the water. And father and son started to sink.

Just then, a gravelly voice called out from the water beneath them.

"What's the trouble?"

A head popped up and, wouldn't you know it, it was the tunny fish that had been with them in the terrible shark's stomach!

"Tunny?" Pinocchio asked. "How did you escape? I thought you had given up."

"I had," the tunny said. "But then I decided to be brave. I followed you. You saved my life and now I shall save yours. Climb aboard my back and I shall soon have you safely to shore."

"Are we too heavy?" asked Pinocchio once they were aboard.

"You're as light as seashells," answered the fish. And in just a few seconds, they had reached the shore.

After thanking the tunny and wishing him well, Geppetto and Pinocchio began to walk. Almost immediately, they came upon two rough-looking characters.

It took Pinocchio a second, but eventually he realized it was Fox and Cat.

After pretending to be blind for so many years, Cat had now really lost sight in both of his eyes.

And Fox—old, thin, and almost hairless— had been forced to sell his fancy, bushy tail for some bread.

They were pathetic. "Help us, Pinocchio!" they begged. "Give us something."

This time, however, Pinocchio was not fooled

by these false friends. He gave them only some priceless advice.

"Remember," he said, "money, and especially stolen money, never bears fruit, in the Field of Wonders or anywhere else!"

"That's it?" Cat asked. "That's all you're going to give us?"

"It's more than you deserve," Pinocchio said, and he and Geppetto continued on their way. They soon came upon a tiny cottage built of straw, and they knocked on the door.

"Who is it?" said a little voice from inside.

"A poor father and a poorer son," they replied, "nearly drowned and now starving and without shelter."

"Come in," the little voice cried.

Geppetto and Pinocchio entered. They looked high and low, but saw no one there.

"I'm up here," the voice cried from above.

There, on a beam, sat Cricket.

"Dear Cricket!" Pinocchio cried happily.

"Oh, now you call me your dear Cricket, but do you remember when you threw your hammer at me and ignored my warnings?"

"I am so sorry," Pinocchio replied. "You're right. You have always been right. I don't deserve forgiveness, but help my poor father, won't you?"

Cricket smiled.

"I will help you both," he said. "I only wanted to remind you that, in this world, we must treat each other the way we wish to be treated."

CHAPTER 18

Pinocchio Becomes a Boy!

ᥴᢞ

When Pinocchio and Geppetto were settled, Cricket revealed that the cottage had been given to him only yesterday by a little goat with blue hair.

"She handed me the keys and went away, bleating sadly. 'Poor Pinocchio,' she said. 'I will never see him again.'"

"So the little blue goat on the white rock, the one who witnessed me being swallowed by the shark, really *was* Fairy!" Pinocchio cried. But where was she now? Still out there, stuck in the middle of the sea? If he wasn't certain that her magic would help her to save herself, he would try to save her, too.

But now he had his father to take care of. Pinocchio carefully made his father a bed of straw and helped the old man lie down. The next step was to get him some nourishment.

"Where can I find some milk?" Pinocchio asked Cricket.

"Three fields away from here lives Farmer John. He has some cows. Go there and he will give you what you want."

Pinocchio ran all the way there, but the farmer wouldn't give him a glass of milk unless Pinocchio gave him a penny.

"I have no penny," Pinocchio said sadly.

"Well, then you'll get no milk."

Pinocchio turned to go.

"Wait a moment," said Farmer John. "Perhaps we can work out a trade. Can you draw water from a well?"

This time Pinocchio didn't protest. He was a changed puppet. "I can try," he said.

"Then go to that well you see there and draw me one hundred bucketfuls of water."

Pinocchio did just that, and one hundred bucketfuls later, he had a warm glass of fresh milk for his father. He had never worked so hard in his life.

From that day on, Pinocchio got up every morning before the sun rose and went to the farm to draw water for the farmer. And every day the farmer gave him a glass of warm milk for his poor old father in return. Geppetto grew stronger and better every day.

But that wasn't all. Pinocchio also took on lots of other little jobs. He helped people with their chores. He made things and sold them. And with the money he received, he and his father were able to keep from starving.

In the evenings, Pinocchio studied by

candlelight from an old, secondhand school workbook that he had bought all by himself with some of the money he had earned.

Before long, he was able to save fifty whole pennies! He decided he would buy a new suit. His was full of holes, and held together with tape.

On his way to the market, Pinocchio ran into an old friend. Why, it was the snail that had lived with Fairy!

"Answer me quickly, sweet but slow snail," he cried. "Where and how is Fairy?"

The snail replied, "Fairy is lying sick in the hospital. She doesn't even have one penny with which to buy a bite of bread."

Pinocchio gasped. Reaching into his pockets, he pulled out his pennies and begged the snail to take them all. He didn't need a new suit. He would give anything he had to help Fairy.

"If you come back in a few days," he added, "I will have even more money to give you."

Inspired by Pinocchio's kindness and generosity, the snail, quite against her normal habit, began to run like a lizard under the hot summer sun.

"Where is your new suit?" Geppetto asked when Pinocchio returned.

"Oh, I decided I didn't really need one after all," Pinocchio replied.

That day, instead of making eight baskets to sell at the market, Pinocchio made sixteen. It was almost midnight when he finished, and he fell quickly into a deep sleep.

That night he dreamed that a beautiful, happy, healthy Fairy kissed him and forgave him. In return for his kindness, and because he had taken care of his father, she promised to give him the thing he had always wanted most.

Awaking and opening his eyes, Pinocchio was stunned to realize that the dream had been real. Instead of being a puppet made of wood, he was finally a real flesh-and-blood boy!

And that wasn't all. Looking around, he found the little straw cottage gone. In its place was a big bed in a comfortable room in a real house!

Jumping down from the bed, Pinocchio saw a new suit, a new hat, and a shiny pair of shoes laid out on a chair.

On the dresser was a note and a leather purse. The note read:

Boys with such kind hearts deserve to keep their pennies.

—Fairy.

Opening the purse, Pinocchio found fifty pennies!

Running to the mirror, Pinocchio could hardly recognize himself. In the glass was a tall boy with big blue eyes, dark brown hair, and a happy, smiling mouth. Why, he was downright handsome!

Pinocchio ran into his father's room, where he

found a man who had also much changed. Several years younger, and looking snazzy in new clothes, he was once again Master Geppetto, the wood carver, already hard at work on his latest craft project.

"How did this happen?" the boy asked in wonder.

"*You* made it happen," Geppetto replied. "When bad boys become good and kind, magic happens."

"And what happened to that poor, naughty old puppet, Pinocchio?"

"There he is," answered Geppetto. And he pointed to a large puppet, leaning against a chair. The puppet's head was turned to one side. His arms hung limp, and his legs were twisted under him.

Taking one last, long look at his old life, Pinocchio sighed contentedly.

"How silly I was," he said. "And how happy I am now that I am a real boy!

And that, my dear readers, was no lie!

What Do *You* Think?
Questions for Discussion

⤍

Have you ever been around a toddler who keeps asking the question "Why?" Does your teacher call on you in class with questions from your homework? Do your parents ask you questions about your day at the dinner table? We are always surrounded by questions that need a specific response. But is it possible to have a question with no right answer?

The following questions are about the book you just read. But this is not a quiz! They are designed to help you look at the people, places, and events in the story from different angles. These questions do not have specific answers. Instead, they might make you think of the story in a completely new way.

Think carefully about each question and enjoy discovering more about this classic story.

1. Why does Geppetto give Pinocchio the three pears? Have you ever given someone something you wanted for yourself?

2. Pinocchio says, "I think danger is something invented by grown-ups, to frighten children who want to have fun." Do you agree? Have you ever done something dangerous?

3. Fairy tells Pinocchio that there are two kinds of lies: those with short legs and those with a long nose. What kind of lie does Pinocchio tell? Do you ever lie?

4. What does Pinocchio discover when he returns to the Field of Wonders? Were you

surprised at Fox and Cat's actions? Have you ever been tricked by a friend?

5. Pinocchio tells the farmer that the weasels tried to bribe him, but says, "As full of faults as I am . . . I refused." What are Pinocchio's faults? Is there something good about him? What do you think are your good and bad qualities?

6. Why does Pinocchio refuse to help anyone on the island of the busy bees? Do you think he was right to expect something for nothing? Are you a lazy person or a busy bee?

7. Why do the policemen think that Pinocchio threw the math book at Eugene? Have you ever been accused of something you didn't do?

8. Pinocchio is persistent in his attempts to get out of the shark's stomach, but Geppetto is willing to give up. Why do you think each feels this way? Which of the two characters are you more like?

9. Why does Pinocchio give the snail all of his money? What is the most generous thing you've ever done?

10. How does Pinocchio finally have his wish granted? Do you think he deserved it? What is your fondest wish?

Afterword

by Arthur Pober, Ed.D.

⁓

First impressions are important.

Whether we are meeting new people, going to new places, or picking up a book unknown to us, first impressions count for a lot. They can lead to warm, lasting memories or can make us shy away from any future encounters.

Can you recall your own first impressions and earliest memories of reading the classics?

Do you remember wading through pages and pages of text to prepare for an exam? Or were you the child who hid under the blanket to read with a flashlight, joining forces with Robin Hood to save Maid Marian? Do you remember only how long it took you to read a lengthy novel such as *Little Women*? Or did you become best friends with the March sisters?

Even for a gifted young reader, getting through long chapters with dense language can easily become overwhelming and can obscure the richness of the story and its characters. Reading an abridged, newly crafted version of a classic novel can be the gentle introduction a child needs to explore the characters and storyline without the frustration of difficult vocabulary and complex themes.

Reading an abridged version of a classic novel gives the young reader a sense of independence and the satisfaction of finishing a "grown-up" book. And when a child is engaged with and inspired by a classic story, the tone is set for further exploration of the story's themes, characters, history, and details. As a child's reading skills advance, the desire to tackle the original, unabridged version of the story will naturally emerge.

If made accessible to young readers, these stories can become invaluable tools for understanding themselves in the context of their families and social environments. This is why the Classic Starts series includes questions that stimulate discussion regarding the impact and social relevance of the characters and stories today. These questions can foster lively conversations between children and their parents or teachers. When we look at the issues, values, and standards of past times in terms of how we live now, we can appreciate literature's classic tales in a very personal and engaging way.

Share your love of reading the classics with a young child, and introduce an imaginary world real enough to last a lifetime.

Dr. Arthur Pober, Ed.D.

Dr. Arthur Pober has spent more than twenty years in the fields of early childhood and gifted education. He is the former principal of one of the world's oldest laboratory schools for gifted youngsters, Hunter College Elementary School, and former Director of Magnet Schools for the Gifted and Talented for more than 25,000 youngsters in New York City.

Dr. Pober is a recognized authority in the areas of media and child protection and is currently the U.S. representative to the European Institute for the Media and European Advertising Standards Alliance.

Explore these wonderful stories in our
Classic Starts™ library.